Cowan

Paddle to Rattlesnake Island

Donna Stewart

illustrated by Lin Souliere

The Brucedale Press

Paddle to Rattlesnake Island is a work of fiction. The characters in the story live only in the imagination of the author and the readers. Details of the setting may bear coincidental likeness to real places, but are used fictitiously.

Brucedale Backpackers # 1
series editor: Lise Gunby

publisher: The Brucedale Press
            Box 2259,
            Port Elgin, Ontario N0H 2C0

National Library of Canada Cataloguing in Publication

Stewart, Donna (Donna C.)
   Paddle to Rattlesnake Island / Donna Stewart ; Lin Souliere, illustrator.

(Brucedale backpackers)

ISBN 1-896922-21-X

   I. Souliere, Lin II. Title. III. Series.

PS8587.T4847P33 2002   jC813'.6   C2002-901535-9
PZ7

Printed and bound by Stan Brown Printers Limited.
This book is created and produced entirely in Canada.

For Peter,
who makes my life
a never-ending adventure.

Acknowledgements

It takes many people to make an adventure happen. First, it takes some dreamers who never lose faith: thank you to my husband Peter, my late mother Maria Simmie, Dean Carriere and Richard Thomas for doing just that. Next, it takes some expertise: thank you to Brent and Joanne Beck. Then, it takes the willing enthusiasts who assist in planning what to take and what to leave behind: my thanks to Denise Cheer, Lillian Cottrill, Janice Greenwood, Lisa Hambleton, Nevan Hambleton, Karen Holgate, Micah Holgate, Helen MacIntyre, Joanne Simmie, Alyson Thompson, Mary Whyte and Brett Whyte. Finally, it takes the skilful passions of those who excitedly set sail together: my thanks to my publisher, Anne Duke Judd, illustrator, Lin Souliere, and editor, Lise Gunby.

Contents

Chapter 1   The New Baby-sitter 8

Chapter 2   Big Boats and Little Boats 20

Chapter 3   Wet Exits..29

Chapter 4   The Story of Rattlesnake Island.........36

Chapter 5   The Water Is Dark 45

Chapter 6   A Missing Person 58

Chapter 7   S'Mores 65

Chapter 8   A Clearing in the Woods 70

Chapter 9   Eskimo Rolls..77

Chapter 10   The Most Important Thing 81

Chapter 1

The New Baby-sitter

Katie and Matt waved.

"Bye Mom! Bye Dad!" Katie yelled, trying to sound happy.

It was Saturday morning, and Katie and Matt's parents were going away for the week-end, again. Every summer, their parents went away with friends for a weekend and Katie and her little brother Matt had to stay behind with a baby-sitter.

"See you Sunday night!" yelled Matt.

Belle started to whine, so Katie bent down to scratch behind her ear. Belle sat down and swished her tail back and forth on the gravel driveway.

"It's okay girl, we'll take good care of you," Katie whispered. "But I'm not too sure about the lady they got to look after *us* this time."

Katie glanced back up the driveway at Roxanne, and Belle licked Katie's cheek.

Roxanne was older than the high school student who looked after Katie and Matt when their parents went out at night, but was younger than old Mrs. Hall. Katie and Matt still talked about how last year Mrs. Hall had snored so loudly that they couldn't sleep until their parents had come home again.

But this lady didn't look anything like old Mrs. Hall. She looked more like the woman who jogged down their road every night after supper.

Then they all heard Roxanne's voice boom: "Hey kids, come on! Help me take my bags into the house."

Katie and Matt walked back up the long lane to Roxanne's car. Katie looked into the back seat. Water bottles, jackets, bungee cords and running shoes lay on the seat beside a suitcase. A book titled *Paddling Basics* lay on the floor. Katie thought it was an awfully messy car, but she would never say so.

Katie liked to think she acted this way because she was polite. But really, Katie was very, very shy.

Roxanne reached far into the trunk and pulled out a pair of in-line skates. The wheels spun as she laid them on the ground. Then she pulled out a skin-diving mask with a dried piece of seaweed stuck on the glass, and one flipper. She stared at the flipper and scratched her head, as though she couldn't remember how the flipper got there. Finally, she pulled out a hockey stick. The black tape around the blade was badly frayed. It seemed that Roxanne used everything she had in her trunk.

Then Roxanne straightened up, put her hands on her hips, and started to mutter. "Now where has it gone?" She stuck her head back in the trunk of her car. Suddenly, a black and white soccer ball flew out and rolled across the grass. As usual, Belle started barking and chased the ball. She chased anything that moved: birds, cats, balls . . . it didn't matter to her what it was. She even chased people, when she really liked them and wanted to play.

"Oh dear, I must have brought that home from school," Roxanne laughed. She scooted across the yard, wrestled the ball away from Belle and tossed it back into her trunk.

"*School?*" Matt and Katie asked at the same time.

"Uh huh. I teach school," she said.

Katie and Matt stared at each other. Roxanne didn't look anything like the teachers at their school!

"I hope you don't mind my asking," said Matt. "But just *where* do you teach school?"

"At a little school in a little town, not far

from here. I don't think you would know it."
She turned her back to him.

Matt looked at Katie. His forehead wrinkled
up as it always did when he was trying to
figure something out.

Hmm, thought Katie, we go to a little
school, in a little town, not far from here.

Katie looked very closely at Roxanne. She
had never seen a teacher who looked like her.
Roxanne wore a white sun visor, a T-shirt that
said "Experience the Thrill! Whitewater
Excursions," and a pair of old worn gym
shorts. Purple and silver sunglasses which
looked like colourful mirrors hung from her
neck on a thick string. She was tanned and her
cheeks were rosy. Most of the teachers Katie
knew wore nice clothes with pumpkin or
candy-cane earrings, and looked tired.

Besides, she thought, all teachers have large
cloth bags full of books in their cars. She had

seen them taking them out to the school parking lot at the end of the day. They did not carry in-line skates and hockey sticks out to their cars. At least she had never seen it happen.

Matt was the one to speak up. "Why do you have all this—this *stuff* in your car?"

"Well," Roxanne said, "I really like sports. I keep my equipment in my car so I always have it with me when I need it—just in case I get a chance to use it. Do you like sports, Matt?"

"A bit," he said softly. He looked down at his feet. "But I'm not very good at most of them."

Roxanne crouched down and looked right at Matt. She was small and pretty. She had friendly brown eyes. She tipped her head sideways, and smiled at him.

"But do you have fun when you are playing sports?" she asked.

"Sometimes," Matt answered, quietly. The corners of his mouth started to turn up.

"Remember that, Matt, because the most important thing is that you always have fun." Then she stood up and disappeared into her trunk, again.

Matt slid his foot back and forth on the ground and grinned at Katie. "Maybe it won't be so bad," he whispered.

Katie was thinking the same thing—that maybe this Roxanne was going to be all right, after all. But it always took Katie a while to warm up to people she didn't know. Her parents always got mad at her. They said she was being rude. She didn't mean to be rude. It was just that she got this awful feeling in her throat when she had to talk to someone she did not know very well. The more people tried to make her talk, the worse her throat felt.

Roxanne pulled out a cloth bag and unzipped it.

Katie tried really hard to ignore the funny feeling in her throat because she really, really wanted to know what Roxanne was doing.

"Um, what are you looking for, Roxanne?" she squeaked.

"My skirt."

"Your skirt?"

"My skirt."

"Why do you need to put on a skirt? I mean—you could always leave your shorts on." Her throat felt as though she had said too much.

"Yeah," said Matt. "I thought Mom said you were taking us to the lake today."

Roxanne didn't seem to be listening. Then she yelled happily, "Here it is!" She pulled out a rather large, bright yellow and black piece of cloth from her bag. Roxanne took the cloth and shook it out for Katie to see. It was made of nylon, had a thick drawstring in the waist and was longer in the front than in the back.

Matt took one look at Roxanne's skirt and gasped.

Katie couldn't help herself. "You are going to wear *that*—to the lake?" Then she slapped her hand over her mouth. She didn't mean to sound rude, it just came out that way.

But Roxanne just laughed at Katie's words. And she had a big, happy belly laugh that made you want to laugh with her.

"No, sillies! This is my *kayak* skirt. I wear it in my kayak. It keeps me in the boat, and helps to keep the water out. We're going to go kayaking this weekend."

Kayaking!

Katie had heard of kayaking before. She knew that a kayak was a narrow boat about the size of a canoe. The paddler sat in a small hole in the middle of it. It floated low in the water. Katie had seen pictures of kayaks in Social Studies last year when they learned about Nunavut. The Inuit were the first people to use kayaks, to hunt seal, long ago.

Katie had also learned that kayakers had to learn to do something called an "Eskimo roll". If they tipped a kayak upside down and wanted to flip it back over quickly without getting out, they needed to know how to roll it back over while they were still in it. Otherwise, they would have to wriggle out of their kayak underwater, so they could come to the surface to breathe!

Just then, a big red truck pulled in their lane. Dust flew from the wheels. The truck pulled a large trailer that carried four kayaks on high racks which swayed back and forth. The driver waved and honked the horn.

The truck came to a sudden stop. A big man

with blondish red curly hair and a big red beard stepped out of the truck's cab. He wore a straw cowboy hat, a red, yellow and orange shirt with fruit on it, black shorts, and rubber flip-flops—the kind with a small strap that fits between your big toe and the next toe.

"G'day folks! And what a great day it is," he said loudly, clapping and rubbing his hands together. "Y'all ready to go?"

Matt and Katie looked at the man, then at the boats, then at each other.

Matt's eyes opened wide. Katie thought she heard him gulp.

Would Roxanne take them out in the lake in one of *those*? With *him*?

But Belle wasn't worried. She took one look at the big man and started to run circles around him. She wagged her tail so hard her back end wiggled.

"Katie, Matt," said Roxanne. "I would like you to meet my friend Sam. He is going to help me show you how to kayak."

Chapter 2

Big Boats and Little Boats

After an early lunch, Katie and Matt sat in the small seats behind the front seats of Sam's truck. The radio was turned up full blast and Roxanne sang along to the words of an old rock-and-roll song she seemed to know well.

Belle hung her head over the front seat, looked up at Sam, and panted happily.

"That dog needs some mouthwash," said Sam.

After a few minutes, Katie leaned toward Matt and whispered. "I don't understand why we have to take kayaking lessons in a swimming pool. Why don't we just go out to the lake?"

"Roxanne said that we have to learn about kayak safety first," said Matt. "I'm scared, Katie." He clutched his lucky rabbit foot in his hand.

Katie tried to be patient with him. He was afraid of so many things. Katie might be nervous about talking to new people, but she wasn't afraid of everything under the sun, as Matt was.

But she felt sorry for Matt sometimes. "Don't be silly, Matt, it's just a little boat. And you know how to swim." She thought it must be awful to be afraid to try new things.

"Well, I passed swimming lessons with flying colours," Matt said. He looked as though he was starting to feel better. "And I *can* swim nine lengths of the pool now."

Katie leaned forward to pat Belle. "And how far can *you* swim, girl?" Katie said. She started to scratch Belle behind the ear again. Belle's tail thumped to the beat of the rock-and-roll.

"Here, kids," Roxanne said, "read this until we get to the pool." She handed them the *Paddling Basics* book Katie had seen in the back of the car.

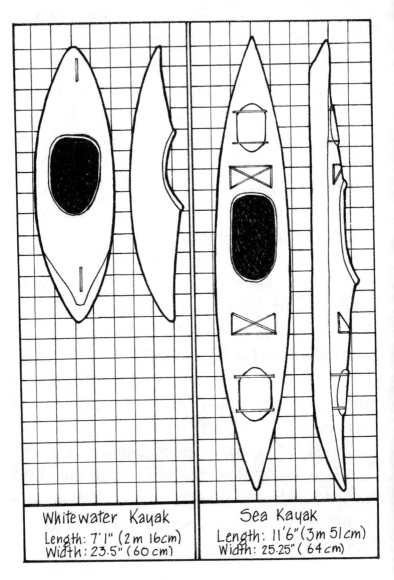

Whitewater Kayak
Length: 7'1" (2 m 16cm)
Width: 23.5" (60 cm)

Sea Kayak
Length: 11'6" (3m 51cm)
Width: 25.25" (64 cm)

Katie flipped through the pages of the book. She stopped when she came to some drawings.

"Hey Matt, look at this."

Katie and Matt looked at the picture.

"Look, there are different kinds of kayaks. This is the kind that's on the trailer." Katie pointed to the picture. "Sea kayaks, it says."

"Er, excuse me," said Matt to Roxanne and Sam, "but what is a whitewater kayak?"

"Hey, hey Big Fella!" said Sam. "Now you're talkin'."

Matt had a funny look on his face when Sam called him 'Big Fella'. He sat up a bit taller.

"Those are for shootin' the rapids, Big Fella. Those kind of boats are built to turn on a dime!"

Matt looked at Sam, confused. "But why would I ever want to turn a boat on top of a dime?"

Roxanne turned down the radio. "Some

people like to try to paddle through fast, rough river waters," she said. "And some people like to learn how to do tricks, so they need a boat that can spin easily. Can you do any tricks on a skateboard, Matt?"

Matt's face lit up. "I learned how to do an ollie this summer!"

"Well, some people learn to do tricks on a skateboard, and some people learn to do tricks in a boat. One trick a whitewater kayaker can learn to do is make his kayak stand up on its end! That trick is called an *ender.*"

With the talk of an ender, Matt went a little white.

Katie forgot about being shy for a moment, and yelled, "Wow! Are we going to learn to do that?"

Matt looked at her as if she had lost her mind.

Katie slid down in her seat and wished she

had kept her mouth shut. But she saw Sam smiling at her in the driver's mirror.

"Now hold on there, Sunshine! You have to learn to walk before you can run." He was laughing. "But you can try out one of my whitewater kayaks today in the pool. You can check out how it spins. We use whitewater boats in the pool, because they are smaller than the sea kayaks."

"We'll teach you the basics first, Katie," said Roxanne. "But you will probably learn to do an ender, someday, if you decide to try whitewater." Katie felt, somehow, that Roxanne didn't doubt for a moment that Katie would do an ender someday.

When they got to the town pool, Belle ran around the truck and Sam in circles, until Katie grabbed Belle by the collar and dragged her to the pool deck.

They had the whole pool to themselves.

Sam's two whitewater kayaks sat on the deck at the shallow end, their noses hanging over the water.

Sam looked down at Belle. She looked up at him and started to wag her tail. But Sam took a wide step away from her on the pool deck. "The most important thing you need to learn before we go out on the lake is how to do a wet exit."

Matt bit his bottom lip. "What's that mean, exactly?" he asked.

"It means that you need to learn how to get out of the kayak if it flips upside down."

"Upside down?" This news didn't seem to make Matt feel any better.

"But first things first," said Sam. "The most important piece of equipment you need when you go kayaking is your life jacket. You need a good one, and one that's the right size for you. Here, try these on."

Katie and Matt put on life jackets that had big armholes and went to their waists.

"Your skirt fits tightly around your waist, and around the sides of the cockpit—the hole you sit in," said Sam. "Now, put on one of these skirts, and I'll show you how to move the foot pegs so you can reach them with your feet and get in."

They each pulled on a skirt, learned how to move their foot pegs, sit in the boat, and make the skirt fit around the cockpit.

"It's very important that you leave the grab loop on the front of the skirt *out*. Do not tuck it inside! You might need to pull on that loop to get out of the kayak when you are upside down. Some people tie something onto the grab loop of their skirt so it will help them to remember to pull it out, and help them to grab it easily underwater."

"I know, I know!" said Matt. "I brought my lucky rabbit foot with me, just in case I needed it. Could I tie it on the grab loop?"

"Now there's a great idea. You go right ahead, Big Fella!"

Katie rolled her eyes. Matt took that smelly old rabbit foot with him every time they did something new.

Sam handed them paddles with a blade on each end.

When Katie and Matt were each sitting in a boat with the skirt pulled tightly around the cockpit, Sam pushed the boats gently off the pool deck and into the water. Then he got in and waded into the water up to his waist.

Chapter 3

Wet Exits

Katie was amazed as she started to glide across the pool. No other boat had ever felt like this. This boat seemed to fit her perfectly. She felt as though she belonged there, on the water, like one of the seagulls she watched bob on the lake. She took a stroke with her paddle.

Katie couldn't help herself. She said "Whee!" as the boat spun in a circle to the left. Right away, she felt silly.

Then she put the blade on the other end of her paddle in the water.

"Whoa there, Sunshine! See what I meant by *you can turn that boat on a dime*?" laughed Sam.

"Katie!" said Roxanne. "You're getting it! Just don't paddle quite so hard."

"But I can't make it go straight," Katie said.

"Whitewater kayaks turn easily. The sea kayak you'll use at the lake is easier to paddle straight."

"Okay," said Sam, rubbing his hands together. "Who wants to flip over first?"

Roxanne looked at Katie and smiled. "You would like to try it first, wouldn't you, Katie."

Katie was glad that Roxanne knew she wanted to, even though she hadn't said it. That was one of the hardest things about being shy. People thought you didn't like them, or that you weren't paying attention, or that you just weren't interested in what you were doing at the time. It wasn't that way at all.

"Um, I guess I'll try," said Katie.

"Hey, you're a little braver than ya look, aren't ya, Sunshine," said Sam. He waded over to Katie and stood right beside her boat.

"Attagirl! Now, there's nothing to it, but

listen up, Sunshine, while Roxanne tells you what to do." Then he winked.

"When you flip over, Katie, I want you to lean forward as though you are trying to touch your nose on your kayak, then pull the grab loop of your skirt to pull the skirt off, then put your hands behind you if you need to, and push your back end right out of the kayak. Okay?"

Katie nodded at Roxanne. Now she was getting nervous. This was a different kind of nervous than when she was asked to talk. This kind of nervous sat right in the middle of her stomach. It was half excitement.

"Go!" said Sam.

Katie took a big breath. Her cheeks puffed up like balloons. She fell sideways, and the bottom of the boat appeared on the top of the water. Within seconds, her head popped up.

"That was easy!" she said. "I just sort of fell out of the boat and did a somersault!"

"That's just what you were supposed to do. Okay Matt, your turn," said Sam.

Matt hesitated. "Listen, maybe I don't need to do this. I'm sure I could get out of this kayak, if I ever *really* needed to." He bit at his lip as though he had burst a bubble of bubble gum and was trying to chew it off.

"Nope. You need to practise this one right here, Matt," Roxanne said. "Right in the pool. You will feel much safer in the lake if you have already practised getting out of the boat in the pool. It's a whole different thing in the lake when you can't see the bottom and the water is cold."

Katie, Roxanne, and Sam waited. Matt was in no hurry to tip his boat over.

Finally, Sam said, "Okay Big Fella, I'm here in the water beside your boat. Now take a big,

big breath, and tip over, and I will go under the water and pull you right outta this here boat if I have to, okay?" He thumped the top of the kayak with his hand. "Just remember to lean forward. C'mon Big Fella. BIG breath. 1, 2, 3, Go!"

Matt's eyes were as big as his cheeks as he tipped his kayak over. Sam's head went under the water too, to make sure Matt was getting out safely. The next thing they knew, Matt's head popped up on the other side of his boat.

"I did it! I did it! It was easy!"

"Good for you, Matt!" said Roxanne. "Now you can have fun too!"

After that, Sam and Roxanne showed Katie and Matt how to paddle properly and how to help each other get back in their boats if they ever flipped their boats over in deep water.

Roxanne said, "Sam, I think they're ready. What do you think?"

"I'm ready!" said Katie. Then she tried to sound a little less excited: "I mean—we need to leave now, don't we, if we are going to have time to kayak before the sun goes down?"

"Yeah," said Matt. "We'd better hurry."

"Don't worry about that. We don't have to be back until tomorrow night," Roxanne said.

"Tomorrow night?" Katie and Matt looked at each other.

"Yes, we're going to camp out tonight," Roxanne said.

"All right!" Katie said. Then she felt silly again, for acting so excited.

Matt groaned. "Will there be any mosquitoes?" he asked.

"No, they aren't too bad out there," said Sam. "But the black-flies have teeth the size of a horse. Just kiddin', kid," he added, rubbing Matt's head. By now, Matt knew when Sam was pulling his leg, and didn't look worried about what Sam had said about the black-flies.

"Where are we going to camp?" Matt asked.

"On the island."

"You're taking us to an island?"

"Yes, we've made plans to go to Rattlesnake Island."

"Rattlesnake Island!" Matt and Katie exclaimed.

Matt turned and looked at Katie. "See! I told you I needed to bring my rabbit foot!"

Chapter 4

The Story of Rattlesnake Island

Matt and Katie stood on the beach. Kayaks, paddles, and gear they had never seen before lay at their feet. Belle barked and ran back and forth on shore, clearing the beach of seagulls.

"*First*, they tell me I have to put on a skirt!" said Matt, arms folded across his chest. "*Then*, they tell me I have to get in a stupid little boat, that is very, very tippy, with a hole in it for a seat. *Then*, they tell me I have to tip it over and try to get out of it if I ever want to take another breath of fresh air! Well, I wasn't too keen on doing any of those things, but I did everything they asked me to do, Katie. But I will *NOT*, I repeat *NOT*, go to any place called *Rattlesnake Island*!"

Matt sat on the sand and sighed loudly.

Katie didn't know what to say to make him

feel better. The truth was, she didn't feel so good about going to Rattlesnake Island, either. But she didn't want to let on to Matt. That would just make it worse.

"They're just snakes, Matt," she tried. "At least they'll warn us with their rattle that they are around."

Roxanne was in the middle of checking equipment, making sure they had everything. She saw Matt sitting on the ground. "What's wrong, Matt?"

"I'm not going."

She looked surprised. "Why? You did very well in the pool."

"I'm just not going, I said."

"Sam and I are very experienced paddlers, and we would not take you out in a kayak if we did not think you were ready. The water is very calm today, there is no wind, and as you can see, Rattlesnake Island is not far from shore."

"I'm not going anywhere that's called *Rattlesnake Island*!"

"Oh, I get it!" said Roxanne, sitting down. "You are worried about rattlesnakes."

"Of course I'm worried about the rattlesnakes. They are poisonous!"

"Yes, they are. But they didn't name the island *Rattlesnake Island* because there are snakes on it."

"Oh," said Matt. He looked confused. "I just figured that must be why they gave it that name."

"Look out at the island." Roxanne pointed. "Do you see anything strange about its shape?"

"Hmm. I see a small island with a tree sticking up at one end."

"If that island were a giant snake, coiled up, what would the tree at the end be?"

"Oh, I get it!" said Matt. "The tree is like the rattle on the end of a rattlesnake."

"Yes! A rattlesnake always puts the tip of its tail, with the rattle on it, up in the air. That is one way you can tell a real rattlesnake from an impostor that just wants to make you believe he is a rattlesnake."

Matt was still suspicious. "How come you know so much about rattlesnakes?"

"I do a lot of hiking around here. I need to know about plants or animals that could be a danger to me. Matt, you have as much chance of seeing a Massasauga Rattlesnake in the woodland near your house as you do on Rattlesnake Island."

"Yeah? Then how come I've never seen one?" said Matt.

"There used to be many more rattlesnakes around here than there are now, but the Massasauga Rattlesnake has now been declared *threatened*. That means that there are not nearly as many of them as there used to be."

"What happened to them?" asked Katie.

"People, mainly. People have been moving in on their habitat. People don't tend to like snakes, either. Fifty years ago, people thought nothing of killing every snake they came across. They hated them. Today, we try to teach people that snakes will usually just slither away—if you give them the chance."

"But how do I know for sure if I see a rattlesnake?" asked Matt.

Roxanne pulled a bundle from the waterproof hatch in her kayak. "I never leave home without this," she said, as she took a book out of a plastic bag and began to turn the pages. "This is a picture of the Massasauga Rattlesnake. And listen:

The Massasauga Rattlesnake is grey with a row of rounded brown-black blotches down the centre of the back and three smaller rows of blotches down each side. Its rattle, at the tip of its tail, is dark brown. The word massasauga *comes from the Indian word for 'great river mouth.' This snake can often be found near water in the spring and fall. In the summer, it is found more often in drier woodland areas or in the cleared area under power lines."*

"Have you ever seen one, Roxanne?" asked Matt.

"Just one. I was riding my bike down a back road on a hot summer day. It crossed the road in front of me. When I was about ten metres away, it rattled its warning, which is really a buzzing sound, and then it moved away."

"What would you have done if it had bitten you, Roxanne?" asked Katie.

"I would have gone to the hospital right away. You do have time to get to a hospital. They would have given me an anti-venom."

Roxanne got up and wiped the sand off her shorts. "I've got to go help Sam," she said. "Feel better, Matt?"

"I'm sure glad they didn't name the island Rattlesnake Island because it's covered in snakes!"

Sam stood beside them, chewing on the end of a long blade of grass. He had been listening and looked as though he was thinking hard about something.

Katie and Matt sat quietly for a moment, looking out over the lake. It was a perfect day. The sun was shining. Katie felt a gentle breeze on her face. The water seemed to be calling her: come and play.

Just then, Belle dropped a slimy stick on Katie's foot and then gave her a wet, sloppy kiss.

Sam walked away.

"Hello, girl. I'm glad you decided to leave those poor seagulls alone," said Katie, scratching Belle behind her ear.

Then, suddenly, Katie thought of something: what were they going to do about Belle?

"Roxanne!" Katie yelled. "What are we going to do about Belle? We can't leave her behind!"

Roxanne looked up from her work. She took

one look at Belle and slapped herself on the forehead.

"Oh no! I forgot about the dog!"

Chapter 5

The Water Is Dark

Roxanne went from kayak to kayak, checking things off on her list. "It's your turn, Katie. Paddle? Check. Skirt? Check. PFD? That's your life jacket. Check. Is your whistle attached to it?"

"Yep! I've got it right here," said Katie. She wished Roxanne would hurry up. She felt pulled by the sound of the waves lapping at the shore. She wanted to get out on the water.

"Is the bailer strapped to your boat?"

"Yep, but I won't need to bail out my boat!" Then Katie looked out over the open water and thought again. "Will I?"

"I sure hope not," said Roxanne. "But it is a good idea to have it, just in case. Now, who has the spare paddle?"

"I do," said Matt. "It's attached to my boat.

And I have the paddle float, as well."

"Good," Roxanne said. "Okay. I have a flare pack and the extra tow line, and Sam is carrying the compass, a knife, and the first aid kit. Check, check, check, check. Oh yes, and Sam is carrying the waterproof matches, too."

"Why do we have to take so much stuff?" asked Matt. He struggled to stow the gear Roxanne had asked him to put in the back of her kayak.

"It is really important that we have all the safety equipment we need, Matt. Just imagine if we got into trouble out on that island, and couldn't get back to shore. Flares could be very useful then."

"But how are we supposed to fit in food, and tents, and sleeping bags?"

"Small packages work best. It is better to use a few small waterproof bags than one large bag."

"No kidding," grumbled Matt. He stopped trying to stuff a bulging green garbage bag into the hole. "I guess I'd better divide this stuff up."

"Good idea. Besides, you are going to have to help me carry some of it. Put some of those things in your boat instead. It looks as though I'm going to need space for an extra passenger in my boat."

Then she looked down at Belle. "You're going to be my stowaway, girl."

Belle looked at Roxanne and thumped her tail in the sand.

Just then, Sam came running back down the beach. He never seemed to get tired. "Well, folks, the weather report says the wind will remain calm and there is no sign of rain. Looks like we've got ourselves the perfect weather for an overnighter. Not only that, Mother Nature has promised us a full moon. Yeehaw! Let's go."

"I wonder if he was ever a camp counsellor," whispered Matt.

Katie giggled. "Only if the camp was in the wild west and they rode kayaks for horses!"

With that, Roxanne, Katie, and Matt pulled

their boats into the shallow water and got in. Then they tried to coax Belle to get into the storage hatch in the back of Roxanne's boat.

"Come on, girl! We can't leave you behind."

Sam looked on and waited. Finally he groaned, "Oh, all right. I'll do it." Sam grumbled as he picked Belle up and put her in the hatch of Roxanne's boat. "Flea-bitten mutt needs some mouthwash." He was still grumbling as he wiped sand and water off the front of his shirt.

After Belle got over the embarrassment of being picked up and stuffed in the hole, she began to look as though she thought she was a queen.

As a group, they started to paddle toward Rattlesnake Island. Katie put her paddle blade in the water, just the way Roxanne and Sam had taught her. She pulled on the water with one blade while she pushed the other end of the paddle forward with her other hand, first on one side, then the other.

Soon, Katie felt as if she was one with her paddle and her boat. Then she was one with the lake, skimming quietly across its surface. Is this how a water animal feels, she wondered? She looked down to the bottom, imagining she was a loon looking for food. She was ready to dive into the warm water.

Between strokes, Sam shouted instructions. "We are going to head for Bird Island first. Some years, this piece of rock is an island, and some years it's under water. This year we're lucky. There is enough of it above the surface that we can stop for a moment and have a rest."

They paddled for another twenty minutes or so to bring their boats in on Bird Island, pulling up onto the rocky piece of land. "I'm glad I have these little rubber slippers on," Matt said. "These rocks hurt the feet!"

Belle jumped from her perch in the boat. She barked and started to clear the seagulls off their own island.

Sam pulled out four apples. The paddlers sat and looked back to the mainland.

"Let's have a picture of the group," Roxanne said. She organized everyone around a boulder, with the shore in the background. It took a while to catch Belle, but they put her right in the middle where she loved to be.

When Roxanne had taken the picture, she asked Katie to hang on to her camera. Katie hung the cord around her neck, then pretended she was taking pictures.

"I'll let you take some real pictures later, Katie. The next time we see something that would make a good picture, you can take one."

"I'm having trouble making my kayak go straight," Matt reported.

"Some boats are more difficult than others

to steer, Matt," said Roxanne. "Why don't you try out Katie's kayak for the rest of the trip?" Maybe more of the bottom of that boat touches the water. If so, it might work better for you."

Matt pulled up the foot pegs in Katie's kayak so he could reach them with his feet, settled himself in the seat, and attached his skirt. He pushed himself off the edge of the island's rock.

"Hey, this is much better!" he said, as he started to paddle.

Katie pushed Matt's pedals back for her longer legs, got in the seat, and attached the skirt. She made sure the grab loop, with Matt's rabbit foot tied to it, was out.

"Your rabbit foot feels disgusting, Matt!" she said. "How long are you going to keep this yucky thing?"

Matt paddled away as if he hadn't heard a word she said.

Katie watched him glide away from her. She wished she could take back what she had just said to her brother, but it was too late.

Matt never made fun of her. He even answered questions for her sometimes, when people tried to push her to talk and her throat felt funny. Katie pushed off the island, feeling unhappy. Why do I do that sometimes? she thought. Matt is the one person in the whole world I can say anything to. What is wrong with me?

Roxanne watched Katie, then turned to Sam, smiling. "Sam, while we're changing boats around, why don't you take mine. Belle would like a new driver for a while." Belle looked at Sam and wagged her tail. Sam made a face. When he called her, she wagged her tail some more, ran around him in a circle, then ran away. She wanted to play. It was a good thing Bird Island was so small, because she couldn't run far. Sam chased her and picked her up and stuffed her into his boat.

Roxanne, Sam and Belle pushed off the rocks too.

Before they knew it, they were close to Rattlesnake Island. They were arriving none too soon. The heat of the day was past, and Katie's stomach told her she had missed her usual supper time.

Sam spoke to Roxanne. "I think we need to hurry up and find us a place to set up camp. That sun is starting to drop out of the sky. This island is small. Why don't I paddle around the west side of the island and look for a good spot? You go around the east side with Katie and Matt. I'll meet you in the middle on the other side. I think that would be fastest."

"Sounds good, Sam. See you in about half an hour. Come on, kids. Let's go this way."

Both Katie and Matt felt their arms getting

very tired. As the sun sank lower and lower in the sky, their stomachs felt more and more empty.

"How far is it?"

"We will stop as soon as we find something that looks like a good spot."

"What are we looking for?" asked Katie.

"Someplace where we have enough shore to pull the boats up, set up our tents, and light a campfire."

"I'm hungry," whined Matt.

"We really do need to hurry. We are running out of daylight faster than I thought we would. We left a bit late," said Roxanne.

"Look! The sun!" yelled Katie.

Roxanne and Matt stopped paddling and looked over their shoulders at the setting sun. It was a huge, orange semi-circle sitting on the western horizon. Shades of pink, red and orange tinted the evening sky.

"Oh Roxanne, can I take a picture?"

"We really need to hurry to shore, Katie. Night time is coming."

"Please, please. Just one! It's beautiful. Look! I've still got your camera hanging around my neck. It will just take a second. And the sun is perfect!" Katie couldn't believe how many words she had said to someone she had just met that day.

"Well, okay. Just one," said Roxanne.

Katie balanced her paddle across her kayak, close to her waist. She lifted the camera and looked through the lens. When she had found the button she needed to push to take the picture, she looked back over her shoulder and focused the camera on the setting sun. Then, suddenly, her sunset started to tip.

"Katie! Sit up!"

It all happened so fast, Katie did not know why Roxanne had yelled at her. All she knew was that Roxanne and Matt were floating in front of her, sideways. It was as if she were lying on a couch, and looking at a TV.

Suddenly, Katie was under the water without having taken the big mouthful of air she had taken in the pool when she had flipped over, on purpose. The lake bubbled around her. It was dark. She did not have the lines of the bottom of a pool to see, and she did not have Sam standing beside her to help her.

All she could see beneath her was the dark, dark, green water of the deep lake.

Chapter 6

A Missing Person

Katie heard a voice inside her head. *Hurry up! Snap out of it!*

Then she knew she had to move fast to get out of her kayak.

Katie remembered what she had been taught.

She leaned forward. She banged around the front edge of the cockpit looking for the grab loop on the front of her skirt. Her hand closed around Matt's rabbit foot, not a minute too soon. She pulled on it, hard. Off came her skirt.

With a shove to the back of the cockpit, Katie was freed from her boat. She somersaulted under her kayak, then her PFD lifted her to the surface.

Air rushed into her lungs.

"Katie! Are you okay?" Roxanne sounded

scared. "I saw you going over, but it was too late for me to help."

"Wow, Katie! Was I ever glad to see you come up!" said Matt.

"It felt as if . . . I was under there . . . forever," said Katie, gasping. She took another deep breath. "Then I found your rabbit foot. It was dangling down. Thanks, Matt. That rabbit foot saved my life . . . "

"I told you I should bring it," he said, pleased.

"I'll never make fun of your rabbit foot again, Matt. I promise."

With the sun setting so quickly, Roxanne and Matt had to use what they knew about kayak rescues to get Katie back in her boat and to shore, before it got dark.

For the first time, Roxanne's voice sounded like a real teacher's.

"Katie, I want you to do what we practised

in the pool. We have to get the end of your kayak up onto the front deck of mine, to empty the water out of your boat. If we are lucky, we won't have to use the bailer."

Katie pushed the front end of her kayak toward the side of Roxanne's boat. Katie was strong. She kicked her feet hard and pushed herself up on the end of her kayak until the other end popped up on top of Roxanne's. It rocked there like a teeter-totter.

"I got it!" yelled Roxanne, quickly slipping the upside-down kayak over the front of her boat. Litres of water poured out.

When she was satisfied it was empty, Roxanne flipped the boat over and slid it back into the water. Then she pulled Katie's boat right beside her own kayak and held on tight, using her paddle across the front deck of both boats to hold Katie's kayak steady.

"Now, Katie, you are going to have to scissor-kick very hard to get your body out of the water high enough to lay your stomach on the back deck of your boat."

Katie kicked as hard as she could, and pulled herself up on the back of her kayak while Roxanne held it steady.

"Now, straddle the boat."

Katie swung her legs around the sides of her boat.

"Now slide your legs into the cockpit, and lower yourself onto your seat."

Katie moved slowly. She prayed that she would not tip the boat back over.

"There! You did it."

"Whew," said Katie, relieved to be back floating on the surface of the water. Though it was July and the lake water was warm, Katie was starting to shiver.

"Come on now, Katie. We've got to get you to shore. It's going to be a long night if we don't get you dried off and warmed up."

Katie had little energy left to paddle, but she did what she had to do. Matt and Roxanne urged her on. "You can do it, Katie. We're almost there!"

The spot they chose to land their boats didn't look perfect, but they decided it would have to do. They pulled their boats on shore and Roxanne immediately started to build a campfire.

"Katie, pull your extra clothes out of the waterproof hatch, and get out of those wet ones. Matt and I will get a fire going."

"But Sam has the waterproof matches!" Matt said.

"I always carry an extra supply in my boat," replied Roxanne. "This is just the kind of event that can easily happen, and I try to be prepared. Having what you need to get a fire started is an important thing."

By now, the sun had set.

"I sure wish that Sam would show up," said Roxanne. "He was supposed to keep paddling around the island until he found us. He should have been here by now. But he will be able to see our fire from the water, or down the shore. It won't be as easy for us to see him if we try to go looking."

They were all very quiet while they ate the stew Roxanne heated up for them.

Roxanne looked worried. All day she had smiled and talked to them. Now she didn't say a word.

In the middle of all that quietness, they all heard a twig snap.

"What was that?" said Matt.

"Likely just a rabbit," Roxanne said. She went back to her meal.

Then they heard something again, moving through the woods, right behind the long piece of driftwood that was their bench.

Katie got up and moved quickly to the other side of the campfire. "Sounds like an awful big rabbit to me."

"Look!" said Matt. "I saw something black and white."

"I wouldn't expect to see a skunk on the island," said Roxanne.

Then Matt started to laugh. "Not unless that skunk has one white ear and answers to the name of Belle!"

"Come, girl," Katie cried. "Come here."

Then Roxanne spoke, in the worst, most serious teacher voice they had heard her use yet.

"Oh no. Where's Sam?"

Chapter 7

S'Mores

"It doesn't make sense that Sam is not with Belle," said Katie. "Maybe his kayak tipped over in the water too, and Belle swam free, but he . . ." Katie hung her head. She felt awful that she had even thought such a thing, let alone said it.

"Maybe Sam just decided to walk around the island instead of paddling, and they got separated. You know what Belle is like. She doesn't always come when you call her."

"Don't worry, kids. Sam is an experienced kayaker. He would always get out of a kayak if it flipped. Besides, if Sam ever flipped over, he would just do an Eskimo roll and be back on the surface. He would hardly even get wet."

"Yeah, Belle wouldn't even have time to get out of the hatch!" added Matt. Then he looked out over the water, and bit his lip.

They all sat back down around the fire.

Roxanne kept looking up and down the shore. The water was like glass. A full moon was rising in the east.

Then they heard the familiar voice of their friend Sam, echoing over the rocks of the shore.

"YOO-HOO! DID ANYBODY HERE ORDER PIZZA?"

Roxanne sighed her relief.

"We're over here, Sam! We're over here!" yelled Katie and Matt.

Soon, Sam's kayak slid onto the shore, and they were together again. They all started talking at once.

"Where were you? I was worried half to death!" scolded Roxanne.

"We knew something was wrong when Belle showed up, and you didn't," said Matt.

"Well, that flea-bitten, four-legged stow-away you gave me took me on a wild goose chase!" he said. "We were just paddlin' along, having a nice time, when that crazy dog decided to chase a momma duck and her babies. She jumped out of the kayak, swam after the duck for as long as she could—the momma quackin' and squawkin'—and then Belle decided to go on shore and take the land route here. I couldn't get her to come for all the dog biscuits in Canada."

"Maybe next time we should leave Belle at home," said Roxanne.

Katie caught Matt's eye. They smiled at each other. Next time?

Sam sat down and enjoyed the stew they had saved for him. Then he pulled from his kayak the ingredients for the best campfire treat Katie and Matt had ever tasted—S'mores: two roasted marshmallows mushed between half a Jersey Milk chocolate bar and two graham crackers.

There are some things about camping that people will remember all of their lives. S'mores, Katie thought, are one of them.

They all sat around the campfire, telling stories. Katie hardly realized that she was talking. She told Roxanne and Sam all about the camping trip they had taken with their parents the year before. She told a ghost story that she had heard only once, and made up the parts she couldn't remember.

Roxanne said it was one of the scariest stories she had ever heard around a campfire. Katie noticed Sam looking over his shoulder into the darkness of the trees.

Matt kept saying how glad he was that he had brought his rabbit foot. Then he told them about all the times his rabbit foot had come in handy since he had won it at the fair.

As they talked, the full moon climbed high in the sky. It was so bright that they could see their shadows on the rocky shore. Roxanne decided to go for one more midnight paddle.

Katie was not too shy to ask if she could go too—just because she wanted to.

The moon above laid a glowing pathway of light on the water. Katie and Roxanne followed it a short way out on the lake. Bats flew through tasty clouds of mosquitoes which hovered close by. Roxanne and Katie watched the bats swoop down and skim the surface of the lake to sip the water with their tongues.

Matt and Sam sat by the fire and watched Roxanne and Katie paddle under the moon. They were two black shapes floating on glittering water and moonlight.

Katie raised the blade of her paddle to wave to Matt and Sam. A bat tapped the tip of her blade as it swooped by. She could almost touch the moon.

Katie wished she could do this forever.

Chapter 8

A Clearing in the Woods

When Roxanne and Katie came back to shore, Sam broke the spell. "Well kids, I hate to be the one to break the news to ya, but all good things must come to an end, and you have to go to bed."

Then he looked around. "Hey, how come you haven't got our tents set up yet?"

"We couldn't because they were stowed in *my* kayak, which *you* were paddling—and *you* were missing," said Roxanne.

"Oh. I didn't see them there. Which hatch were they in?"

Roxanne thought for a moment, then she sighed deeply. "I guess I'm not too well prepared this time, am I, kids? I took them out of the hatch when I put Belle in, and forgot to put them somewhere else. They are back on shore.

I guess we'll just sleep under the stars tonight."

"On the bare ground?" asked Matt.

"I guess you don't have much choice now, do ya, Big Fella," said Sam, scratching his head. "Heck, I've been sleepin' under the stars for years. We're just lucky the weather is good. At least we have our sleeping bags. With a plastic sheet beneath us, and one on top to keep off the dew, we'll be just fine."

Roxanne still made Katie and Matt brush their teeth, even out in the middle of an island.

They slept under the moon that night.

And they thought they were alone.

* * *

The next morning, Matt woke up first. He got out of his sleeping bag and put on his rubber kayaking slippers. They had slept late. The morning sun was already warm.

He walked down to the shore to wash his face. When he came back, Katie was awake too. She wiggled her fingers and mouthed the word *hi*.

Matt motioned to Katie to come, then put his finger to his lips: "Shhh."

Katie slipped out from under her sleeping bag and damp plastic sheet as quietly as she could. She pulled on her slippers too, and followed Matt. Belle walked after them, down the shore.

"Where are we going?" Katie asked, when they were far enough away.

"Let's just look around a bit," Matt said. "I'm just wondering what is in the middle of this island."

Most of the island was thick bush, too thick to walk through, unless you were a dog. Every once in a while they tried to push into the brush, but the branches soon became too thick to get through and Katie and Matt went back to the shore.

"Let's follow Belle," said Matt. "Maybe she will find a way that we can also get through. She did come out of the bush last night."

Sure enough, Belle led them into the woods. They pushed away tree branches to follow her. Soon they found themselves in a small clearing in the middle of the forest.

The sun beat down in this little spot. Katie noticed the warmth on her skin after the cool dampness of the woods.

"What a place for a secret fort!" said Matt. "Just think what you could do back here. You could build an entire village."

Katie ran across the clearing. It felt good to be on a patch of grass again, after a whole day of stepping on nothing but stones. She spun around to tell Matt, and what she saw beside him made her freeze.

"M-M-M-Matt!" she whispered. "D-D-D-Don't move!" Katie pointed. "R-R-R-Rattlesnake!"

By the time Matt had turned his head in the direction Katie had pointed, the buzzing sound of the rattlesnake's warning had filled the small clearing. And the dark brown rattle of the Massasauga was unmistakable, pointing toward the sky.

Belle started to bark. She barked and she barked and she barked. She wanted to play with the rattlesnake. She put her head down and wagged her tail.

Katie worried that the snake might bite Belle, but Belle didn't get too close. She just barked and jumped, wanting to play.

Suddenly, Roxanne and Sam stumbled out of the woods into the clearing. "What's going . . ." Roxanne did not finish her sentence. "Belle! Come here!"

For the very first time in two days, Belle did as she was told. When she left the snake and trotted to Roxanne, the frightened rattlesnake slithered away into the woods.

"Am I ever glad to see you!" Katie said.

"Me too," said Matt.

"You know," said Sam, rubbing his hands together, "they don't call this place Rattlesnake Island for nothin' folks."

Katie and Matt were speechless.

Same pulled them close. "I thought maybe Roxanne was way off base on that one, but I didn't want to scare ya, and I didn't want to hurt Roxanne's feelings, ya know." Sam rolled a blade of grass between his teeth. Then he got a faraway, cowboy sort of look in his eye.

"Ever heard of Whiskey Island? Folks try to say that they called it 'Whiskey' 'cause when you looked out at it, the island was the shape of a whiskey bottle lying on its side. Well, I'll tell ya, they were just dead wrong about that one, too. Yes, sirree, dead wrong!"

Katie and Matt started to giggle.

"Yup, they call this place Rattlesnake Island for good reason."

"What's so funny?" Roxanne asked.

"Nothin' much," said Sam. "Just givin' the kids a little history lesson." He winked at Katie and Matt, tipped the front of his straw cowboy hat, and headed back out to the shore.

Chapter 9

Eskimo Rolls

Katie and Matt did not mind when Roxanne told them that they were going to leave the island as soon as they had finished breakfast and packed up their gear.

This time, Sam tricked Belle into coming with him by pretending he was going for a walk. Then he picked her up and put her in the hatch of Roxanne's kayak.

As they paddled across the lake, back to Bird Island, Katie noticed that she had sore muscles in her shoulders and arms in places where she hadn't even known she had muscles. Even so, she was proud that she could paddle a kayak all by herself. The sore muscles almost felt good.

During the rest stop on Bird Island, the

paddlers ate a snack and played at the water's edge. Belle continued to chase birds.

Sam and Roxanne showed Matt and Katie how to do an Eskimo roll. They taught them how to flick their hips to begin flipping their boat back over, and where to place their paddles on the surface of the water so they could roll themselves back up. They made it look easy.

"I think you two are just showing off," said Matt.

Roxanne grinned. "But we're having fun! Remember that, Matt. The most important thing is that you're having fun."

Katie and Matt both tried to do a roll, too. Roxanne and Sam got in the water and helped them by flipping their boat back over, but neither Katie nor Matt could do it alone.

At the same time Matt was trying to learn to do that Eskimo roll, he was having more fun than he had had all summer. And while Katie was getting tired, she still wanted to keep trying.

"Don't worry!" said Roxanne. "You'll get it. I know you will. No one gets it the first time. It took me a whole summer to learn."

"Took me a whole year, Sunshine!" added Sam.

Finally, tired and happy, they left Bird Island and headed for shore. This time, Belle stowed away in the hatch of Katie's boat.

Twenty feet from shore, Belle could take the lure of the seagulls on the beach no longer. With only one warning bark, she leapt from Katie's kayak into the water. She was chasing those gulls, again.

When Katie's boat started to tip, she was ready.

Her cheeks puffed up like balloons. She went under. She hung there for a moment, upside down, thinking. She placed her paddle on the surface and looked up at her blade. Then she snapped her hips and pulled hard. Before she could say "rabbit foot," she had rolled back up to the surface and was sitting upright.

The cheers of Sam, Roxanne, and Matt rang in her ears.

She had done it. She had done her first Eskimo roll.

She was a real kayaker now.

Chapter 10

The Most Important Thing

Katie and Matt watched the back of Sam's truck and trailer become a small dot at the end of their road, then disappear.

"Will we ever see Sam again, Roxanne?" asked Matt.

"I hope so. Where do you want to go next time—Wolf Island?" She smiled.

"No way," said Matt. "But I'd like to go kayaking again."

"I'll see what I can do."

Katie and Matt's parents had already said good-bye to Roxanne in the house, and thanked her for giving Katie and Matt the "little kayak lesson" and for taking them on "that little island trip."

Katie and Matt hadn't told their parents *everything* that had happened on the weekend.

When it came to their parents and baby-sitters, Katie and Matt had learned that some things are best left unsaid.

Roxanne stuffed all the equipment she had used on the weekend back into the trunk of her car; her kayak skirt, her paddle, and her *Paddling Basics* book disappeared into the trunk.

"Roxanne? Will we ever see *you* again?" asked Katie.

"Well, it's funny you should ask that, Katie," said Roxanne.

"Why?"

"Because your parents just asked me if I could look after you again some time."

"All right!" Katie exclaimed.

Matt shuffled his feet on the ground, looked up at Roxanne and grinned.

Roxanne got into her car and slammed the door. Rock-and-roll music spilled out of her window. "Then again," Roxanne said, "I might just see you at school."

Matt's jaw dropped to the ground. "Why are you saying that? Are you going to be our teacher? What school *do* you work at?"

"You never know, Matt, you just never know."

Roxanne started to pull away. Katie couldn't resist another peek into the mess Roxanne called her back seat.

Katie elbowed Matt. "Look, Matt, look! Do you see what I see in the back seat?"

Matt stretched his neck. "Is that the top of a SCUBA tank?"

Katie said, "No, I mean on the other side. It looks like the tip of a ski."

Matt shook his head. "Why does she carry all that stuff in her car?"

"You know what she said about always being prepared," answered Katie.

Katie and Matt waved good-bye to their friend.

At the end of the driveway, Roxanne stuck her head out the window and yelled, "Remember! The most important thing is that you have fun!"

Katie and Matt watched the back of Roxanne's car disappear down the road. She left them in a cloud of summer dust, swirling with the sound of a rock-and-roll song.

About the Author

Donna Stewart brings her enthusiasm for outdoor sports and teaching to writing for young children. From her home on the Bruce Peninsula, she has many opportunities to play in and on the waters of Georgian Bay and Lake Huron.

"*Paddle to Rattlesnake Island* was inspired by my experiences kayaking with my children," she says. "Our family has been so very lucky to live in a beautiful place, where we can have fun outdoors year round. I wish every child could enjoy summer from the warm seat of a boat, or on the moonlit shore of an island. I believe stories have the power to inspire real life—maybe readers who can't go kayaking now will someday find themselves outdoors, gliding across a lake."

Donna's stories for adults have appeared in one journal and the anthologies *Shorewords* and *The Brucedale Family Reader.* She received a grant under the Explorations Program of the Canada Council to complete an as-yet-unpublished collection of stories.

Donna teaches at the Bluewater Technology Centre in Hepworth, Ontario.

She is a Friend of CANSCAIP and a member of The Canadian Children's Book Centre.

Watch for the next adventure of Katie, Matt, Roxanne, and Belle.

Skiing in Black Bear Park

Katie listened.

The forest was quiet. The only sound they could hear was the scrape of their winter boots on gravel dug up by a snowplough.

The road curved. Katie's flashlight beam showed a wooden building.

"Listen!" whispered Katie. "I hear something."

A sudden movement in the tree beside them made Katie and Matt freeze.

Brucedale Backpackers #2
Skiing in Black Bear Park
by Donna Stewart

Look for it at your bookstore or library.